Christmas Carols for Cats

Julie and John Hope

www.cato9tales.com

Contents

THE TWELVE DAYS OF CATMAS

Sing to:
The Twelve Days of Christmas

On the first day of Catmas there came a gift from me
A tear in your precious settee

On the second day of Catmas there came a gift from me
Two headless mice and a tear in your precious settee

On the third day of Catmas there came a gift from me
Three fur balls
Two headless mice and a tear in your precious settee

On the fourth day of Catmas there came a gift from me
Four feathered friends
Three fur balls
Two headless mice and a tear in your precious settee

On the fifth day of Catmas there came a gift from me
Five fur-ry things
Four feathered friends
Three fur balls
Two headless mice and a tear in your precious settee

You've got the idea now? Come sing along...
...Six strays a-spraying...
...Seven trays a-brimming...
...Eight fish heads reeking...
...Nine fleas a-leaping...
...Ten toms a-wailing...
...Eleven kittens mewling...
...Twelve vet bills coming...

❄ ❄ ❄

WE WISH FOR THE FAM'LY GOLDFISH

Sing to:
We Wish You a Merry Christmas

We wish for the fam'ly goldfish
Why in bowl and not in our dish
We wish for the fam'ly goldfish
To bring us good cheer

Of longing we sing for food to appear
We wish for the fam'ly goldfish to bring us good cheer

We long for the hamster squeaking
Along to his house we're sneaking
We long for the hamster squeaking
A snack we revere

In wonder we sing why live food is here
We long for the hamster squeaking a snack we revere

We're sick of the budgie chirping
Let's eat him and all be burping
We're sick of the budgie chirping
Each day of the year

The food that can talk we do not hold dear
We're sick of the budgie chirping each day of the year

❄ ❄ ❄

WE THREE MOGGIES DEFIANT ARE

Sing to: We Three Kings of Orient Are

We three moggies defiant are
Something's wrong the door ain't ajar
This ain't humane, please to explain
'Ceedingly quite bizarre

Refrain: O – flap to hinder flap to fright
Flap to push with all your might
We are freezing, can't be squeezing
Through a door that's rather tight

Flattens fur and pinches the ear
Traps the tail and bangs on my rear
It's not sporty when you're portly
Wish it would disappear

Refrain

Keep on howling someone will come
Door is opening let's have some fun
We're so willing this is thrilling
Through our cat flap we run

Refrain

COLLAR BELLS

Sing to: Jingle Bells

Collar bells, collar bells
Scares the birds away
O I hate this stupid thing
It's with me night and day

Refrain: Stalking through the grass
Jingling sound of brass
Caught nothing for a week
Feeling like a freak

Collar pink, collar pink
O I really pray
I can wriggle out of this
The guys all think I'm gay

Refrain

Collar smells, collar smells
Catching all the fleas
Everyone just treats me like
I have a bad disease

Refrain

❄ ❄ ❄

RING RING   RING RING

O COME ALL YE WAKEFUL

Sing to: O Come All Ye Faithful

O come all ye wakeful
Find a nice location
A warm knee, a settee
Relax in the sun
Sleep on your sweater
Though your coat is better

Refrain: O let us yawn and snore some
Keeping one eye open
O let us yawn and snore some
Ou-r reward

O come and be gracious
Your bed is so spacious
O choose well and snooze well
And don't make a fuss
Sofa and armchair
Cover them with shed hair

Refrain

O sleep where you're able
Bookshelf or a table
A good nap on broad lap
Will serve just as well
Life has such meaning
Paws in air and dreaming

Refrain

HOLY FRIGHT

Sing to: Silent Night

Holy fright, torment in sight
Great alarm, all's not right
Round the bend to the kennels we ride
Bars on windows and nowhere to hide
Sleep without any pe-eace
Weep for early release

Food so bland, trays of sand
No TV, no settee
Fleas all gone and there's nothing to do
No fat mice or a bird I could chew
Sleep without any pe-eace
Weep for early release

Made a pal, O what a gal
She is good for morale
Touching noses there's plenty to say
But tomorrow she's going away
Sleep without any pe-eace
Weep for early release

Nowhere to play, brushed every day
Think I'm going home today
Please come early or walls I will climb
I'll look surly and treat you like slime
Sleep without any pe-eace
Weep for early release

❄ ❄ ❄

THE FIRST SLOW YELL

Sing to: The First Noel

The first slow yell for you as you lay
Asleep in the morning on Christmas Day
O do not snore please get out of bed
It's seven o'clock and I haven't been fed

Refrain: O Yell O Yell O Yell O Yell
Feed me at once or I'll make your life hell

To lay a-bed is an awful disgrace
Get up right now or I'll sit on your face
My furry paw 'neath the covers will crawl
Fill up my bowl or I'll caterwaul

Refrain

Your last big chance, now give us a break
I've clawed at your nightshirt you should be awake
I'll niggle and naggle, be ever so rude
For nothing else matters when I want my food

❄ ❄ ❄

O LET US CLOWN & CAUSE MAYHEM

Sing to: God Rest Ye Merry Gentlemen

O let us clown and cause mayhem
Upon you we will prey
To overcome the tedium
We shred your new duvet
Let's rummage in the nice clean clothes
So much to do today

Refrain: O finding some mischief is joy, mischief is joy
O finding some mischief is joy

We overturn the rubbish bin
Across the floor to spread
With dirty paws we wander in
Clean places we must tread
Here's a furball that's a-coming
Leave it on your bed

Refrain

O hand us down from this tall tree
We'll cry for all we're worth
The fire engine it will come
As we jump to the earth
Up the curtains we'll be running
There will be much mirth

Refrain

Let's play a game of hide and seek
To find us you must guess
Best humour us before we try
To leave this house a mess
We know you really like the teasing
Come on now confess

Refrain

GOOD CLEAN WHISKERS

Sing to: Good King Wenceslas

Good clean whiskers wash them out
Comb them straight and even
Face is next now turn about
Back paw, forepaw and then
Lightly on the bit that's white
Shining like a jew-el
Looking good now do it right
Beauty and renew-ew-al

Nap a while then clean a tail
Dry it by the heater
Not too long to make it stale
Smell a little sweeter
Sing a washing song of fish
Birds and hot persu-al
Check reflection in your dish
'Fore it fills with gru-u-el

Was it whiskers was it ear
Feel I've done so little
Top of head or fluffy rear
Running short of spittle
Can't remember what I've done
Have a quick review-al
Better start again for fun
Or face ridi-cu-u-le

❄ ❄ ❄

WHILE I DID WASH MY SOCKS

Sing to: While Shepherds Watched

While I did wash my socks that night
I quickly looked around
The human of my house crept up
And turned me upside down

"Dear cat", said he, "O do not dread
We're going to the vet"
I'll cry and scream and carry on
And make your car seat wet

It's terrible to wait in line
The place is full of mutts
O awful creature loved by man
Tongues out to lick their butts

Well shocking things did happen there
He held my tail aloft
And squeezed me where I cannot say
Then asked me please to cough!

O misery the needle's out
The forepaw he did shave
My claw shot out and he did shout
I showed him who was brave

All glory be we're going home
I'm in an awful mood
I'll turn my back on everyone
And sulk 'til I get food

AWAY FROM ALL DANGER

Sing to: Away in a Manger

Away from all danger not covered at all
There's sitting a turkey I'm hoping to maul
There's nobody looking, my fate I will seal
And don't you be thinking that guilt I will feel

Now I am so clever I am a good thief
I have to choose quickly 'tween turkey and beef
A fish in a bright dish or cream I will lick
And eat it all quickly until I am sick

I know it's forbidden, I know it's the truth
To eat on the table is really uncouth
But this is so tempting I don't really care
And blame the soft humans for leaving it there

❄ ❄ ❄

BARK! THE HAIRY SCARY THINGS

Sing to: Hark, the Herald Angels Sing

Bark! The hairy scary things
Story of the stress they bring
Fear the feather duster wild
Hate the screaming of that child

Refrain: Bark! The hairy scary things
Story of the stress they bring

Thunder lightning – stay inside
Vacuum cleaners make me hide
Wind in chimney, sirens wail
Slam of door and trapping tail

Refrain

Tripping up when mutts they chase
Jumping wall and losing face
Leaves that jitter, clocks that ding
Horses skitter, kettles sing

Refrain

Funny noises, wind-up mouse
Strangers coming to my house
You must think I'm such a clot
But my nerves are really shot

❄ ❄ ❄

THE AUTHORS

Julie Hope was born in Sheffield, Yorkshire in 1952. She qualified as a furniture designer and spent many years in this profession. This not being an occupation with a high content of fun and flippancy, Julie found a convenient outlet in illustrating, cartooning, and writing whimsical verse. Her cartoons, birthday cards and Christmas cards were always of enormous delight to family, friends and colleagues. In 1982 Julie emigrated to South Africa where she later met and married John Hope, an electronics engineer. One night in 1995 the two of them wrote the songs for Christmas Carols for Cats in the back of a small notebook and on bits of paper serviette whilst dining in a Chinese restaurant in Johannesburg.

Christmas Carols for Cats was published by Bantam in 1996, but to Julie's disappointment the publisher insisted on using their in-house illustrator. Subsequent books, Nursery Rhymes for Cats, and Christmas Crackers for Cats followed the same format. In 1997 Julie and John and their four cats relocated to Oxfordshire, UK.

In 2007 John wrote his first full length book, Nine Lives, handsomely illustrated by Julie, which they self-published in September 2010. Sadly, Julie died later the same month and it was John's intention to keep Julie's work alive by continuing to write books and online media for whimsical cat lovers, using her large archive of unpublished illustrations.

John F. Hope was born in Johannesburg, South Africa in 1958 and began writing anthropomorphic stories about animals at age six, encouraged by his grade school teacher. Some of this was frowned upon by the headmaster because said stories failed the test of political correctness, even in 1964. John's other passion in life was electronics, which he enthusiastically embraced at age eight and cemented over the next few decades by becoming an electronics engineer of some skill.

In 1990 he met and married Julie, and the whimsical synergy that resulted from this union led to the publishing of three books by Bantam, Christmas Carols for Cats, Nursery Rhymes for Cats, and Christmas Crackers for Cats.

John passed away suddenly in September 2016, six years after his late wife, Julie - to the day.

Andrea Hope was born in Baildon, Yorkshire, and studied graphic design. She enjoyed a long career in this field, working in advertising, TV and package design before switching to a career in travel in the nineties. John and Andrea met and married in 2011 and another creative union developed with Andrea producing the covers for her husband's books. They lived together with their cats in Longhope, Gloucestershire until John's untimely death.

Andrea has subsequently maintained the cat9tales website, regularly posting John's astute observations, whimsical cat stories and a secret language of cats: Cat Speak. You can read these wonderful stories here: **www.cat9tales.com**

Andrea has since returned to working full time in photography, and art, producing hand drawn pastel pencil portraits of pets, babies and children.

See Andrea's work here: **www-pi-artstudios.com**

❄ ❄ ❄

OTHER BOOKS BY THE AUTHORS
Christmas Crackers for Cats
Nursery Rhymes for Cats
Nine Lives
Hatching Discordia

Printed in Great Britain
by Amazon